Mission: Lullaby

TOMMY DONBAVAND

WALKER
BOOKS

First published 2014 by Walker Books Ltd
87 Vauxhall Walk, London SE11 5HJ

10 9 8 7 6 5 4 3 2 1

This book has been typeset in Helvetica and Journal

Printed and bound in Great Britain
by Clays Ltd, St Ives plc

British Library Cataloguing in Publication Data:
a catalogue record for this book is available from the British Library

ISBN 978-1-4063-3163-9

www.walker.co.uk

www.fangsvampirespy.co.uk

For Sue and Kev

MPI Personnel

Agent Fangs Enigma
World's greatest vampire spy

Agent Puppy Brown
Wily werewolf and Fangs's super sidekick

Phlem
Head of MP1

Miss Bile
Phlem's personal secretary

Professor Hubert Cubit, aka Cube
Head of MP1's technical division

Wednesday 0911 hours: **Houses of Parliament, London, UK**

59 ... 58 ... 57...

Special Agent Fangs Enigma licked the tips of his sharp vampire teeth in concentration and then very carefully began to loosen the final screw in the cover of the bomb. He worked the screwdriver slowly, knowing that any sudden movement could cause the device to explode. Hearing footsteps running across the floor of the deserted House of Commons chamber, he looked over his shoulder to see a werewolf running towards him.

"Everyone's evacuated, boss," said the werewolf and fellow secret agent Puppy Brown.

Puppy and Fangs both worked for intelligence agency Monster Protection, 1st Unit, aka MP1. "The place is empty," Puppy confirmed.

"And the bomb squad?"

"Six minutes away."

Fangs glanced down at the red LED timer on the bomb: *45 ... 44 ... 43...* "We don't have that long," he said.

"Lucky we were heading back to HQ when the bomb was found," said Puppy. The entrance to MP1 Headquarters was in Parliament Square, which was right opposite the House of Commons.

"Yep," said Fangs. He pulled the screw out. "This is what I call lucky." He paused to wipe the sweat from his brow. Then he pressed his hands to the metal case and made to lift it off.

Puppy placed a hand on his arm. "Are you sure you know what you're doing, boss?" she asked. "MP1 training doesn't include classes in defusing bombs."

"Trust me." The vampire smiled. "These things

all work the same way. Inside here will be a circuit board and a mass of wires. You never cut the red wire – that's a booby trap set by the bomb maker. The thing will explode if you do that. The green wire is fake. It's just put there to confuse you."

"Which leaves?"

"The blue wire," said Fangs. "You always cut the blue wire." After taking a deep breath, he slid the cover off and they both leaned in to peer inside. As predicted, there was a circuit board and a virtual bird's nest of wiring.

Only, all the wires were yellow.

Fangs blinked. "I have to admit I wasn't expecting that."

The LED timer counted down a few more seconds: *33 … 32 … 31…*

"What do we do now?" hissed Puppy.

"Well," said Fangs, "we haven't got enough time to get outside, and the bomb squad will still be fighting its way through the traffic." He produced a pocket knife from inside his cape and then winked at Puppy from behind his sunglasses. "What say we give it a go?"

"And if we get it wrong?"

"Then at least we go out with a *bang*."

27 … 26 … 25…

Fangs used the tip of the knife to lift up one of the yellow wires to see where it connected to the circuit board. It was impossible to tell.

"What do you think?" he asked.

Puppy shrugged. "I've never seen anything like it," she admitted. "Your guess is as good as mine."

"That sounds like the closest thing we have to a plan."

19 … 18 … 17…

Puppy's sensitive werewolf ears twitched. "I can hear sirens approaching," she said. "The bomb squad is almost here."

"Just in time for the fireworks," said Fangs. He began to touch each of the identical wires in turn with the knife. "Eeny … meeny … miney … mo."

A wire chosen, he twisted the knife and began to cut.

12 ... 11 ... 10...

"Boss," whispered Puppy. "Just in case... Thanks. I've loved every minute of working with you at MP1."

Fangs wrapped an arm around his friend's shoulders and gave her a cuddle. "Me too." He grinned.

Then he cut through the wire.

Nothing happened. The readout continued to count down.

7 ... 6 ... 5...

"It was worth a try," said Fangs. He threw his vampire cape over himself and Puppy before clicking a button sewn inside the lining that turned the fabric solid. It would provide some protection against the explosion, but it was unlikely to be enough.

3 ... 2 ... 1...

BOING!

Then silence…

After a few seconds, Fangs released the switch and his cape reverted to soft, black material. He peeped out from beneath it. "Where was the BOOM?" he asked. "I was expecting a BOOM, not a—" He stopped mid-sentence.

"What is it?" asked Puppy, emerging from beneath the cloak. She turned to look at the bomb, and her eyes widened.

Broken pieces of circuit board lay scattered around, with charred lengths of smouldering wire still attached to it here and there. But that wasn't what she and Fangs were staring at.

A large metal spring coiled up from the centre of the device and there, wobbling gently at the top, was a single black glove.

TOP SECRET
MP1 Mission File #6
Mission: Lullaby
Report by: Agent Puppy Brown

The MP1 security ogre put his hand out to stop us. "Passes," he grunted.

Fangs whipped open his vampire cape to reveal his security pass, which was clipped to the breast pocket of his jacket.

I showed the ogre my pass and he let us into the lobby of MP1. I put the "bomb" we had recovered from the House of Commons down on the desk. Its glove bobbed from side to side at the top of the spring as though it was waving. The ogre eyed it suspiciously. "I think it likes you," I quipped – only to get a stony expression in return.

In all the time I'd been working here, I couldn't remember the guard ever smiling.

"I'll just pop it through the scanner," I said, moving the "bomb" onto the short conveyor belt of the machine that would X-ray it and check for residual traces of magic.

Getting the device from the House of Commons to HQ hadn't exactly been easy. The local police had wanted to take it for further examination, but we'd received orders from our boss not to let them have it. MP1 agents had made the device safe, so MP1 would be the ones to examine it.

I had carried the device very carefully. We still weren't sure whether there were explosives packed into its base. One bump and it could go off in my paws!

Bomb or no bomb, you might be forgiven for thinking that the sight of a vampire and a werewolf crossing the road in the middle of London would cause a bit of a panic. However, since the supernatural equality laws were passed, creatures like Fangs and I were a common sight all over the world. Among the crowds behind the police cordon on Parliament Square, I spotted a school bus of young skeletons and a zombie collecting money for a charity which specialized in reuniting the undead with their missing limbs.

The warning lights above the security scanner lit up a mixture of red and yellow, telling us that the device contained some traces of magic but, thankfully, no live explosives. I picked up the glove again. We walked on and a few moments later, we were outside Phlem's office.

"FANGSH!" In a whirlwind of wild, grey hair, Phlem's secretary, Miss Bile, scurried over to greet my boss. Fangs smiled pleasantly as the aged banshee helped him off with his cloak and carefully hung it up on the coat rack.

"I HAVEN'T SHEEN YOU IN AGESH!" she bellowed, spraying the carpet with globs of saliva. "OR, AT LEASHT, IT SHEEMSH THAT WAY."

My boss took the banshee's hand in his and gently kissed it. "You were never far from my thoughts, Miss Bile," he crooned.

The secretary's eyes rolled back in her head and she fainted to the floor, her head wedging neatly in a waste-paper basket. She still had a smile on her semi-conscious face as I helped her back to her desk.

The intercom barked into life. "Enough of the nonsense, Enigma. Get in here now."

We entered Phlem's office. I set the device down on his desk. He bent to peer at it with dull, green eyes. No matter how many times I saw the head of MP1, it was always something of a shock. The rumour was that he was the only swamp beast ever to have survived away from the legendary black lagoon. Now his home was here in London, and his job was to run MP1 – an organization which was the thin, green line between ordinary humans and the world's greatest criminal *monster*minds.

Fangs settled back into an armchair and accepted a drink – a glass of milk with just a drop of human blood. I chose orange juice

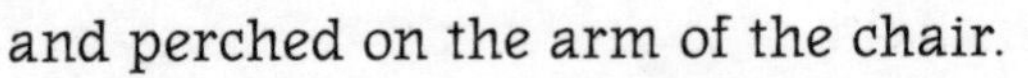

and perched on the arm of the chair.

"Gloves," Phlem gurgled as he dropped a couple of ice cubes into his own drink – a healthy serving of liquid mud. "They're everywhere."

"Gloves *plural*?" I asked. "You mean there are more?"

Phlem nodded. "The mayor discovered one in his fridge at six a.m. Her Majesty the Queen was wearing a single black glove when she woke up, and this was waiting on my desk when I arrived this morning." He slid open a drawer and took out a black leather glove. It was identical to the one which had sprung out of the device.

"Well, they're not getting around by themselves," said Fangs. "Someone must have a *hand* in it." He smirked, then he mumbled, "Suit yourselves," when neither Phlem nor I laughed.

"Have we got any leads?" I asked.

"Yes," said Fangs. "Anyone we can *finger* for the crimes?"

"It's not good news," said Phlem.

"Well, whoever it is, they'd better not try to *palm* the blame for what they've done onto anyone else," said Fangs.

Phlem glared at him. "Be serious, Agent Enigma. Take a look at this..."

On the screen of his computer was the image of a single black glove on a green background and the words "Glorious League of Villainous Evil (GLOVE)."

I gasped. "League... You don't mean...?"

"Yes," said Phlem. "The bad guys are joining forces."

"What do we know about this GLOVE organization?" Fangs asked.

"Not much," admitted Phlem. "The website is encrypted, but we've had a team working on breaking the code for the past few hours. They'd just called to tell me they'd cracked it when you arrived. Let's take a look, shall we?"

He clicked on the image of the glove and then entered a long password into the resulting pop-up window. After a few seconds, the page changed. A gallery of photographs appeared – photographs of a few of the worst super-villains in the world.

"That's Carlos Trumpet," I said, pointing to a picture of a skeleton.

General Rot

Carlos Trumpet

"He's wanted for stealing a jewel-encrusted skull made by that artist Damien Hirst," I added.

"And General Rot," Fangs said, pointing at the disfigured face of a zombie. "He threatened Australia with a missile made of his own body parts."

My eyes flicked over the rest of the screen in horror. "Arnold Goose, Betty Flame..."

Fangs was equally shocked. "These are some of the top names from our wanted list."

"Correct, Agent Enigma," glugged Phlem, after downing his glass of mud.

Arnold Goose

Betty Flame

"The idea of these criminals sharing information and resources doesn't bear thinking about."

"They could do anything," said Fangs quietly. "Individually, they're a nuisance, but nothing we can't stop. Together, though, they could take over the entire world."

"But who's organized all this?" I asked. "Who set up GLOVE and got all these villains in one place?"

"He calls himself Mr Big," said Phlem.

"And that's all we know." He scrolled to the top of the screen. The cursor hovered over a silhouette, underneath which was written "Mr Big".

"As you can see, Mr Big's identity

remains anonymous. We've never managed to capture him on camera. We need to fill in the blanks about his identity and what he's planning," said Phlem, "especially now that GLOVE is making itself known to the world. We have to find out what its plans are."

"So what do we do?" I asked.

"*You* won't be doing anything, Agent Brown," Phlem replied. "Do you think I could trust you two after the mess you've just made with that bomb? Hand over your MP1 security passes, please. You're both fired."

Fangs leapt to his feet. "Fired?" he demanded. "On what grounds?"

Phlem clicked a button on his computer keyboard and the image changed to show CCTV footage of me and Fangs trying to disable the bomb. The sound quality wasn't great, but I could hear my boss choosing which wire to cut.

"Eeny ... meeny ... miney ... mo."

Fangs sat down again. "Ah, you saw that bit, then?"

"MP1 has eyes, ears and tentacles everywhere, Enigma," Phlem said. "Your tomfoolery put hundreds of lives at risk."

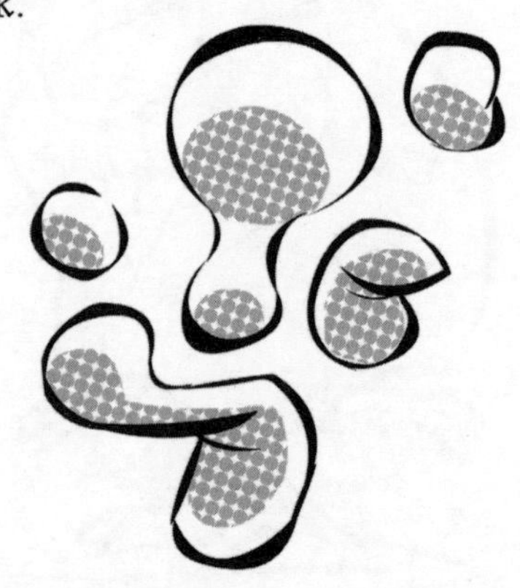

"But..." began Fangs.

"No buts," snapped Phlem. "I showed you the GLOVE website to demonstrate the dire threat the world now faces. And I don't think you two are up to the job of protecting it any longer." He flicked a switch on his intercom. "Security. Please escort *former* agents Enigma and Brown off the premises."

I dropped a handful of change onto the counter of the small cafe. "A glass of milk and an orange juice, please."

"I don't suppose you have any human blood, do you?" Fangs asked hopefully. "A-Positive, if possible."

The man behind the counter didn't reply. He just snarled and rang up our order. "Bert!" he called into the kitchen. "One orange juice and one milk – plain."

Fangs and I found a table and sat down. "I can't believe this is happening," I said.

"Me neither," said my boss. "I'm the world's greatest vampire spy! They can't get rid of me."

"They already have," I reminded him. "And me, too."

"It can't be the way we dealt with that bomb," said Fangs. "It has to be something else. Something Phlem isn't telling us. If you hack into his computer, we may be able to find out the real reason he fired us."

"I can't," I said. "My laptop and utility belt were confiscated on the way out of the building."

I turned to watch the raindrops run down the cafe window and saw my own hairy reflection staring back at me. What would I do now that I was no longer a spy? I supposed I'd have to go back to school, and that wouldn't be a very pleasant experience.

You've probably read stories that tell you werewolves only transform once a month at full moon but live totally normal lives in between. Well, I'm the exact opposite. Something went wrong during my first transformation and I ended up permanently stuck with the fur and the fangs – except for once a month when I turn back into a girl.

My school had some supernatural pupils, including a couple of werewolves, but unless you were with them at full moon, you never saw them as wolves. The fact that I was a wolf all the time made school very difficult. For instance, I wasn't allowed near the stoves in cookery class in case my fur caught alight, and I was banned from playing volleyball in PE because my claws kept puncturing the balls. I was miserable.

Everything changed when I was recruited by MPl. Within days, I was learning to hack into computer systems, drive all manner of bizarre vehicles – and I was working with the world's greatest vampire spy, Fangs Enigma (at least, that's what it says on his business card). Now all that was over.

"Boss..." I began, but then I stopped myself. Fangs wasn't my boss any more. He was just a vampire I happened to know. Tears welled up in my eyes, and I quickly wiped them away (one of the few uses of hairy hands). "I don't know what–"

But I didn't get to finish my sentence because a figure in a white apron and chef's hat scurried over to our table. "One glass of orange juice for the werewolf..." he said, setting my drink down in front of me. "And a glass of milk, with just a dash of A-Positive blood – for sir."

"But the man behind the counter said..." I stared up at the chef and found a pair of friendly and familiar eyes smiling back at me from behind a set of square-framed glasses.

"Cube!" I cried. It was Professor Hubert Cubit, the head of MPI's technical division.

"Ssshhh." Cube pressed a finger to his lips as he sat down. Then he removed his white hat to reveal a square head.

Early on in life, the professor had realized that facts and information only ever come in square things. "Books, computers, filing cabinets – all square and all filled with knowledge," he told me during my first week of training. "Tennis balls, potatoes and scoops of ice cream – all round and hardly any knowledge in them at all."

Determined that he would also be stuffed with information, the young Hubert built a tight-fitting wooden box to wear like a hat at all times, so changing the shape of his head as it grew, from a useless sphere to a fact-filled square. It is for this reason that he is now known as "Cube". He earns his living as MPI's top brainbox – literally. And, right now, I couldn't have been happier to see his cuboid cranium.

Even Fangs seemed to be delighted he was here. "Kind of you to stay in touch," he said, "but you'd better watch your back. You don't want to be caught talking to us. We've been disavowed."

"Disavowed?" I asked.

"It's a spy word. It means no longer trusted by the secret government agency which employed you," Fangs explained. "I heard it used in a movie."

"I'm not worried about being seen talking to either of you," said Cube, kindly. "Mainly because you *haven't* been disavowed."

"Yes, we have," said Fangs. "We were thrown out of the building, and Jeff the security ogre frisked me on the way out. He's got really rough hands."

Cube checked that no one was watching our table and then he pulled a small laptop computer from the pocket of his apron. "I think you'd better see this," he said, opening it up. Phlem's face appeared on the screen.

"Agents Enigma and Brown," he said. "My apologies for putting you through that."

"I don't understand, sir," I said. "What's going on?"

"We have to get someone on the inside of GLOVE right away," Phlem replied. "We need to discover their plans."

Fangs's brow furrowed. "You want us to go undercover? Why didn't you just say so?"

Phlem shook his head and the tendrils of slime that hung from the corners of his mouth jiggled. "Your reputations precede you both. Even in disguise, you could be

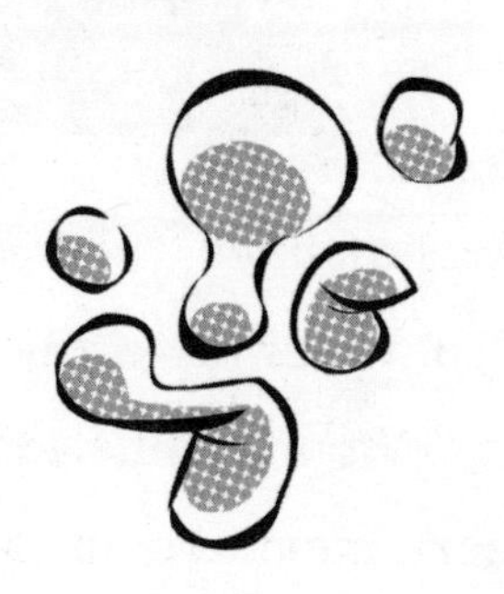

recognized. But we need you – our best agents – to infiltrate GLOVE somehow."

Things were starting to make sense. "So you fired us to give us the perfect motive for revenge on MPI. The world has to think that we're turning bad."

"Exactly," said Phlem.

I grinned, thrilled to be back on the case again. "So what's the plan?"

"We've identified a villain who wants to earn membership of GLOVE," Phlem explained.

"I need you to convince him to hire you both as henchmen."

"I get that bit," said Fangs. "But what was all that nonsense back at Headquarters? Surely we could just *pretend* we'd been sacked?"

"Someone left a black glove on my desk this morning, Enigma," said Phlem. "That means GLOVE has someone on the inside here at MPl. Beyond you two and Cube, I don't know who I can and can't trust. Your exit from MPl had to look real."

"Including our reactions," I said.

"Precisely, Agent Brown," said Phlem. "The mole could have access to your MPl records and so, from this moment, everything you ever used as part of your jobs has been confiscated. You no longer live in MPl accommodation, have access to MPl vehicles or permission to use any of Cube's gadgets. You're going to have to complete this assignment on your wits alone."

Fangs leaned back in his chair and put his hands behind his head. "That shouldn't be too much of a problem..." I caught him just before the chair tipped over and he crashed to the floor.

"So who's the target?" I asked. "Who do we have to convince to hire us as goons?"

The image on the screen changed to a freeze-frame shot of a troll.

"This is Derek Dopper," said Phlem. "A small-time villain with dreams of joining the major leagues. The tech boys found an email he sent to GLOVE asking for membership, but the organization won't take him seriously. That's where you two come in."

"In what way?" Fangs asked.

"You have to help him come up with a scheme villainous enough to get him membership of GLOVE. Once he's inside, he'll be invited to GLOVE HQ and, as his henchmen, you will go with him."

"And then once we're inside, we can tell you the identity of Mr Big and his plans," I said. "It's brilliant."

"So what do we know about Derek?" asked Fangs. "How did he come to our attention?"

"GLOVE wasn't the only organization he contacted," said Phlem. "Watch."

Cube pressed another button, and the video started to play. The troll made a trumpet shape with his hand and sang a fanfare. "I trust I have your attention now, MPI! I am Derek Dopper, and I am the baddest villain you guys have ever met."

He pulled what he might have thought was a scary face, but which actually made him look like he desperately needed the toilet. Then he continued: "Unless you pay me the sum of one million pounds, I will inject hot chilli sauce into every acorn in Britain! Squirrels everywhere will go crazy, and before long they will join with me to create a Squirrel Army—"

Suddenly, the door to the room opened, and an older, female troll entered, carrying a vacuum cleaner. "I've got to do your room, Derek," she said, spraying a bottle of air freshener.

"Mum," Derek coughed. "Don't spray that stuff in here. You know it affects my allergies." He took a couple of puffs from an asthma inhaler.

"I have to clean, Derek. I can't have the place getting dusty! Go and play outside for half an hour."

"I'm not *playing*, Mum. This is serious stuff! And now you've interrupted me, I'll have to start all over again."

"Pfft! You shouldn't be hanging around indoors. You should be out there, trying to find a job."

"But, Mum..."

"Don't you 'But, Mum' me! Now, get out while I clean up. I told you not to bring those crisps up here last night."

There was a hiss of static and the video ended.

Fangs and I exchanged a glance. "I think we may need more than just our wits," I said.

"We want Junction thirty-two," said Fangs, reading the map. We were driving to the guesthouse in Blackpool where Derek Dopper lived with his mum.

It would usually take us a while to track down the headquarters of a villain, but Derek Dopper had helpfully written his return address on the back of the envelope when sending his "Squirrel Army" DVD to MPI Headquarters. I couldn't quite believe he would want anyone to see that video.

I could only presume that he'd sent the wrong copy.

As we didn't have access to an MPI car, my dad had lent us his old runaround. It wasn't exactly up to Fangs's usual standards, and he kept fiddling with the controls. He'd just switched on the windscreen wipers. I turned them off as he began to play with the air-conditioning settings. The fur on my face wafted as it was treated to a sudden blast of ice-cold air.

"What are you doing?" I demanded.

"Looking for the cocktail cabinet," Fangs replied. "I need a drink."

"There is no cocktail cabinet," I said. "That's just in MPI cars."

"Oh," said Fangs. He paused and then said, "Massage controls for the seats?"

I shook my head.

Fangs shrugged, but didn't reply. He sat in silence for a few moments, twiddling his thumbs. I continued concentrating on the road, wondering how we were going to introduce ourselves to Derek when we arrived. We'd have to–

"Are we there yet?" Fangs asked.

"What?"

"Are we in Blackpool yet?"

"No," I said. "We've got another eighty-six miles to go."

Fangs sighed dramatically. "This is taking for ever," he moaned. "We'd have been there by now if Phlem had let us take the jet."

"He can't exactly say he's disavowed us, and then let us borrow a plane."

"He could say we stole it..."

"And then we'd have the police on our tail as well," I pointed out. "If you're bored, why don't you listen to the radio?"

With another sigh, Fangs switched on the car stereo. Cheesy 80s pop music blared out. "Oh, no, no, no..." He twisted the dial. The next station blasted out the latest hip-hop hit from the top of the charts. "No chance." Fangs kept turning the dial.

Eventually, he settled on a news programme. The presenter was in the middle of discussing something very familiar. "... urgent government security meeting following the discovery of a hoax bomb in the House of Commons this morning. Thankfully, the bomb squad was able to make the device safe, and it was later—"

"Hey!" Fangs yelled at the radio. "The bomb squad didn't even get there in time. We were the ones who dealt with it!"

"I know that, Fangs," said the presenter, "but we can't let GLOVE know you were ever involved."

The car swerved as I took my eyes off the road to stare at the radio in surprise. "Did the news reader just reply to you?" I asked.

The exit to a service station was coming up, so I indicated and turned off the motorway.

"Yes, he did," replied the radio. This time it was a voice I recognized. "And, frankly, he's been waiting for you to turn the radio on for ages now."

"Cube," I cried. "That's you, isn't it?"

"The one and only."

Fangs was still staring at the radio in bemusement. "When did you get a job as a newsreader?" he asked.

"I'm *not* a newsreader," Cube replied. "I'm simply using the FM frequency to connect your radio speaker to the mobile phone I slipped into Puppy's pocket in the cafe."

I put a hand in my pocket and pulled out the phone. "I thought Phlem said you weren't allowed to give us any gadgets," I said, handing the phone to Fangs.

"Well, it's not really a gadget, is it?" said Cube.

"And I wanted you to have a way to stay in touch. Nice little number, that one. I installed a voice-scrambler chip inside it."

"Voice scrambler?" I repeated.

"Yes," said Cube. "It allows you to disguise your voice. Just choose a setting from the app, and you can sound like you're a human, goblin or harpy – or just about anyone or anything else, in fact."

"That will be why we didn't recognize your voice on the radio at first," said Fangs.

"Precisely. I remotely activated the scrambler before I started to broadcast via your radio."

"How does it work?" asked Fangs.

"You just launch the app," said Cube. "You'll find it on the communications screen. You don't always need a radio frequency to make it work, of course."

"Thanks for your help, professor," I said. "It's good to know you're there if we need you."

"You're very welcome," said Cube. "I'd better sign off before anyone finds out I'm helping you."

There was a hiss, and then the radio signal went dead. I started the car and headed for the service-station exit.

"It was good of Cube to help us like that," I said. "Wasn't it, boss?"

There was no reply.

"Boss?"

Fangs was too busy fiddling with the phone to answer me. He tapped the screen a few times, and then spoke into the mouthpiece. His voice came out of the car radio sounding like that of an old-time radio announcer. "We now return you to the amazing adventures of Fangs Enigma, the world's greatest vampire spy! It was a cold and frosty morning when the grave, yet disturbingly handsome vampire dropped into the alleyway behind the armed thugs..."

He was lost in a world of his own making. I sighed and pulled back onto the motorway. We still had over 80 miles to go...

* * *

We pulled up outside the guesthouse at just after 7 p.m. "*Caribbean Dreams*," Fangs read the sign above the door. "More like a nightmare, if you ask me. We're not really staying here, are we? Isn't there a five-star hotel somewhere nearby?"

"It'll be fine," I said, getting out of the car. "My mum and dad used to bring me to Blackpool every year to see the illuminations. We always had fun."

With an expression of disbelief, Fangs joined me in getting our luggage out of the boot. "You will let me know when the fun starts, won't you?"

We knocked on the door and it was opened by the female troll we'd seen in the video. It was Derek's mum. She was wearing a flowery apron and a pair of pink rubber gloves. "Hello," I said, cheerily. "Your sign in the window says you have vacancies. Could we possibly book two rooms for a couple of days?"

The landlady looked us up and down suspiciously. "Here for a holiday, are you?"

"Something like that," I said. "There's a convention in town for fans of a vampire-detective series. We've come to get some autographs." Fangs's story about the amazing adventures of Fangs Enigma had come in useful, after all.

"All right," said the landlady. "Follow me..." She led us into the house and up to the first landing. "These will be your rooms," she continued, gesturing to a pair of doors at the end of the corridor. "You'll get hot water from seven to seven-thirty, and breakfast is served on the dot at eight. There's a shared bathroom on the next floor up, just along from my son's room. Make sure you don't go peeking in his room, though. He doesn't like nosy parkers."

Fangs whipped off his sunglasses and grabbed the landlady's hand. He kissed the leathery skin. "We promise to abide by the rules of your charming hostelry," he crooned. "Miss...?"

The troll scowled. "Dopper," she said, pulling her hand away. "Doris Dopper."

"Enchanted to meet you, Doris."

"Is your son at home?" I asked as innocently as I could. "It would be nice to have someone local who could show us around."

"He's at work till midnight," said Doris.

"Really?" I said. "What does he do?"

"He's in show business, or so he reckons. He calls the numbers at one of them bingo arcades in town – Bingo Bongo."

The arcade was packed. End-of-season tourists pumped handfuls of coins into slot machines, or clacked a plastic puck back and forth across rows of air-hockey tables. Wherever we turned, there were flashing lights, ringing bells and electronic beeps.

Fangs looked around with a barely disguised sneer. "You realize I'm more used to spending time at the casino in Monte Carlo, don't you? Staying in five-star hotels and travelling first class."

I did my best to hide my smile. "Ah, but that was back when you were a secret agent. Now, we're just a pair of henchmen for hire, trying to find work."

"I know," said Fangs, "and it's depressing me."

"Well, if you don't think you can play the part of a lowly henchman for a couple of days..."

Fangs bristled at the accusation. "Of course I can," he said defiantly. "Never let it be said that Fangs Enigma is not in touch with the common man." With that, he strode up to a nearby change booth and smiled widely at the cashier. "I will have milk on the rocks, with a twist of lemon, please."

The woman stared back at him open-mouthed. "You what?" she asked.

"I'd like a glass of milk," Fangs explained.

"Are you taking the mickey?"

"It's just his sense of humour," I said, sliding a ten-pound note across the counter. "Can we have some pound coins, please?"

"It might be best if I do the talking for the time being," I suggested, as I led Fangs away.

"Up to you," he replied. "I just want to find Derek and get out of here. The flashing lights and constant noise are giving me a headache." He glanced around. "Where is he?"

I pricked up my sensitive werewolf ears, trying to pick individual sounds out of the hullabaloo. I could hear a child crying over a dropped ice cream, a man bragging to his friends that he was about to win the jackpot on a slot machine, the

PFFT! PFFT! PFFT!

of air-powered rifles firing on the shooting gallery, and then...

"Seven and two, seventy-two... On its own, the number three... Two fat ladies... Eighty-eight..."

"That's him," I said. "This way..."

Fangs followed me to the back of the arcade, where people were playing bingo on multi-coloured boards, each hoping to fill a single line or get a full house and win a prize. And calling the numbers, his huge troll body squeezed into the caller's booth, was Derek Dopper. He was on a plinth so he could see over a mountain of "Kiss Me Quick" hats and models of Blackpool Tower.

"That's him,"

said Fangs. "What do you suggest we do?"

Before I could answer, a cry rang out: "Bingo!" Someone had filled their card and claimed a full house.

"I think we should play it cool, boss," I said. "Let's sit in on the next game."

Fangs sighed. "You want me to play bingo? It's hardly a challenge, is it? Not like the skill required for poker, or the quick judgment you need for blackjack."

"Eyes down for a single line," said Derek into his microphone as we each sat behind a bingo screen. "And your first number is ... one little duck, the number two..."

I felt Fangs stiffen in the seat beside me. "I've got that number," he hissed. "What do I do?"

"Just cross it off," I said. "Now you only need the other four numbers on that line to win."

Derek's voice boomed out again. "Eight and nine... Eighty-nine..."

"I've got that one, as well," squeaked Fangs excitedly.

"Six and one... Sixty-one..."

"I haven't got that one."

"Key of the door... Twenty-one..."

"I've got that one," exclaimed Fangs. He continued to shout out as each number was called.

"Five and seven... Fifty-seven..."

"Nope."

"Seven and four... Seventy-four..."

"Gah."

"Two fat ladies... Eighty-eight..."

"Oh, come on."

"Clickety click... Sixty-six..."

"Yes!" Fangs was almost vibrating with excitement. "I just need forty-three," he said.

"And the next number out is..."

"Forty-three," Fangs whispered. "Forty-three, forty-three, forty-three, forty-three, forty-three..."

"Four and three... Forty-three..."

"YES!" Fangs leapt up and punched his fist into the air. "BONGOS!"

"I think you mean 'bingo', boss." I smiled.

"BINGO!" he said. "What do I win?"

I checked the board above Derek's chair. "Well, one line wins you a stick of Blackpool rock, but the numbers will have to be confirmed first."

Derek was watching us. "Ready?" he asked.

Fangs nodded eagerly, and then turned to me. "What do I do?" he whispered.

"You read out the numbers in your winning line, and the caller will check them off on his board."

"OK," said Fangs. "I think I've got the hang of this bingo lark now." He read out the first number. "Number two... One little duck."

Derek smiled as he checked his own board. "One little duck, the number two..."

I couldn't remember seeing Fangs ever look this proud. "Twenty-one... Key of the door..."

"Key of the door, twenty-one..."

The other players were chuckling at Fangs's enthusiasm now. "Seems like we've got ourselves a wannabe bingo-caller," said Derek into the microphone. "Your next number, please..."

Fangs slid the next tiny door open. "Four and three..." He paused for a moment, trying to remember if there was a special call for this number, then he said: "Squirrel army."

Derek's face fell. He stared at us. "Here," he said, nervously. "I know you two from somewhere..."

"Not us," I said with a smile. "We're just tourists, up here for a vampire-detective convention."

"Although," Fangs said, "he might know us because we are ... I mean, were ... world-famous spies – before we were disavowed, of course."

"Sshh!" I hissed – but it was too late.

Derek had leapt up and was running for the exit. I gave chase.

"What about my stick of rock?" Fangs cried after me.

"I'll buy you another one," I yelled. "Come on."

By the time my boss caught up with me, Derek was at the front of the arcade. He crashed out through the double doors and turned left onto the promenade, pushing people out of the way as he went. After charging through a group of girls out on a hen night, he ducked into a building on his left. "He's gone in there," I said, skidding to a halt outside the entrance to the attraction. "Into the haunted-house ride."

The doors had been painted to look like iron gates at the entrance to a creepy crypt and above were the words:

HOUSE OF HORRORS

They had been daubed in dripping red paint. Fake cobwebs fluttered in the breeze and a plastic skeleton hung from the window of the ticket booth next door. Low moans and screeches echoed from a speaker fixed to the wall.

I slapped the rest of my change down on the counter, behind which sat a bored-looking man in a zombie outfit. "Two, please – as quick as you can."

We crept along a narrow corridor lit only by ultraviolet bulbs. The special effects were rubbish. Manic laughter rang out from hidden speakers, steam shot out in front of us, and ribbon brushed our cheeks. Before long, we found ourselves walking through a graveyard. Mist rolled over the bumpy ground, oozing between plastic headstones that jutted from the fake grass.

"This place is stupid," moaned Fangs. "I mean – who'd be scared of stuff like this?"

Suddenly, a fist burst up out of the grave nearest to us. Fangs screamed – properly screamed, like a four-year-old who had just found a spider in the bath. He stamped on the hand, shattering the plastic and bending the metal underneath until all that was left

was a jagged stump that whirred as it rose and fell above its damaged motor.

"I thought that might have been Derek about to attack you," said Fangs, trying to regain his composure. "Remind me to pay for it on the way out."

"Are you sure you're OK to go on?" I asked.

"Of course," said Fangs. "That thing just took me by surprise. Bound to happen when your senses are as keen as mine."

"All right," I said. "But let's try to stay quiet. We don't want Derek to hear us."

As we left the graveyard, a cardboard ghost popped out in front of us. (Fangs ripped it down from its wire.) Then a sarcophagus swung open to reveal a moaning mummy. (Fangs punched it in the face.) Dozens of plastic cockroaches rained down on our heads. (Fangs jumped up into my arms and cried for his mum.)

I sighed. "Look, boss," I said, "why don't you wait outside–"

Fangs's scream cut me off. "There's a monster behind me."

I turned to see a mannequin standing in the shadows behind us. "It's just another prop," I said.

"I knew that," said Fangs, straightening his bow tie. "I just wanted to see if you did, Puppy." Then he spun round on one leg and struck the model in the stomach. "Hi-ya!"

"OOF!"

"Puppy..." Fangs said slowly.

"Yes, boss?"

"Did that plastic exhibit just say 'OOF!'?"

"Yes, it did, boss," I replied as Derek Dopper stepped out of the shadows and clamped a hand on our shoulders.

"I think we need to have a little talk," he growled. Then he dragged the pair of us through a door that had been hidden behind a fake spider's web and into a brightly lit store room, filled with boxes of Halloween props and rolls of spare tickets.

I blinked at the sudden change in light. I needed to think fast if we were going to convince Derek to take us on as his henchmen. "Listen," I said. "It's OK – we're on your side."

"My side," spat Derek. "But you're from MPl! You're Fangs Enigma and Puppy Brown. And he hit me." He pointed at Fangs and rubbed his stomach. "That really hurt."

"Sorry about that," said Fangs. "I thought you were a dummy."

"And now you're insulting me as well!" Derek shoved us into two wooden chairs. Then he grabbed a coil of fake human intestines from a hook on the wall and began to tie us up.

"We *were* with MPl," said Fangs as the troll tied his hands behind his back. "But not any more. We hate MPl now. We've been disavowed."

Derek's brow furrowed. "Disavowed?" he repeated.

"Fired, sacked, given the boot," I added as Derek secured my wrists to the chair with a string of fake guts. "They got rid of us – after all we'd done for them. They tossed us out like yesterday's leftovers."

Derek stepped back to stare at us, and the top of his head brushed the ceiling tiles. "I don't believe you."

"Trust me," said Fangs. "I wouldn't be here if they hadn't taken the keys to my luxury MPl flat."

"So what are you here for?"

"We want revenge," I said. "We want to teach MPl a lesson for doing this to us."

Fangs nodded. "Puppy's right. And the best way to show those goody-goodies in London that we mean business is to swap sides and work for a villain like you. Show them what a threat to society you really are."

Derek looked surprised at this. "*I'm* a threat to society?"

"That's how we see you," I said. "But MPI don't. They didn't take your brilliant squirrel-army plot seriously, did they?"

"No, well ... I accidentally sent them the wrong video...."

I knew it!

"But that video was a work of genius," I said.

"It was?" Derek and Fangs said together.

"Of course," I said. "Arranging for your mum to burst in like that and make it look as though you were some sort of fool gave MPI a false sense of security. Made them think you were just another wannabe villain – an amateur – whereas we know you're a genuine danger to mankind."

Derek straightened up, a look of pride washing over his face.

"Yes, I suppose I *am* pretty dangerous..."

Fangs looked as though he was about to disagree, so I kicked him in the shin and continued. "Bingo-calling isn't the career for a great super-villain like Derek Dopper," I said. "You should be ruling the world from a hollow volcano somewhere."

Derek's eyes grew misty as he imagined his ideal lair.

"And now that MPl think you're a laughing-stock, you are ready to strike," I said. "They'll never see you coming. You really are a genius, and a criminal mastermind like you needs henchmen. Henchmen who despise MPl as much as you do."

"That's true," said Derek. "But where would I find henchmen like that who would want to work for me?"

"I've no idea," said Fangs.

I kicked him again.

"We'll do it," I said. "Hire us as your henchmen, and we'll help you earn membership of GLOVE."

Derek's large eyes narrowed. "How do you know I want to join GLOVE?"

I thought quickly. "Which scheming super-villain wouldn't want to join it? Let us help you earn membership, then, together, we can get revenge on MPl."

Derek paced the room as he thought this through. "You want to work for me?"

"That's *exactly* what we want," I said.

"And you'd have to do what I ask, no matter how scary?"

"You're the boss," said Fangs, finally catching on. "Although I think you'll find there isn't much that scares me..."

Fangs gripped the microphone with trembling fingers as a rock-guitar intro played, and the name of a song flashed up on screens all around the bar:

Dying Is Forever

The audience of supernatural creatures cheered as Fangs began to sing along nervously:

"Dying is forever,

Unless you are a zombie,

Then take some advice from me..."

Derek and I were seated at a table near the back of the room, watching him. We were squeezed in between a pair of drunken gnomes and a giantess who elbowed me in the ribs every time she took a sip from her bucket of beer. Derek had insisted on coming to his favourite karaoke bar and then made Fangs and me choose songs to sing from the zombie disc-jockey's list of titles, just as he had.

"This is brilliant," cried Derek over the music. "I normally have to come here by myself, but now that you're my henchmen, I can order you to sing with me any time I want." He took a blast from his inhaler. "I might even get you to stop the DJ from using his smoke machine. It really affects my allergies."

"Don't you think we'd be better spending our time thinking up evil plans to impress GLOVE?" I asked.

"That's exactly what I am doing," replied Derek. "I come up with my best ideas while I'm singing karaoke. Ooh, it's all happening now! It won't be long till I've moved into an evil lair of my very own. My mum will be really proud of me."

On the stage, Fangs was looking worried. I'd seen him battle bad guys, chase villains and foil the wicked schemes of some of the greatest criminal *monster*minds the world had *ever* seen, but I'd never seen him look as uncomfortable as he did right now.

The music was blaring, and the flashing lights were directed straight into his eyes. A harpy – her hair a writhing mass of hissing snakes – danced wildly at the front of the stage while he tried to concentrate on his words. When the song was finally over, the DJ – a local radio celebrity called Crisp Boils – called for a round of applause. Fangs left the stage.

"I'm next." Derek beamed, jumping out of his

seat and knocking my glass of orange juice over. The troll raced to the microphone, insisting that Fangs give him a celebratory high-five as they passed each other.

The title of Derek's song flashed up onto the screens:

Zombie Feasting Time

Fangs slumped into the empty chair beside me as the song started. "I am never doing that again," he grunted. "I'd rather swim through a tank full of hungry sharks in a suit made out of raw meat." Fangs rubbed a hand over his face as Derek began to sing. "Tell me I didn't sound as bad as that."

"You did well, boss," I said. "You had at least one fan down there."

Fangs glanced at the harpy, who was now dancing along happily while Derek sang.

"I think she'd dance to the sound of the fire alarm if it went off," said Fangs. "That's an idea, actually. Let's set off the alarm and get out of here."

"We can't," I said, patting his arm. "We have to find a way to get into GLOVE."

"Well, I can't think straight with 'Karaoke Ken' screeching

up there," said Fangs. "I never thought I'd say this, but I want to go back to his mum's guesthouse and..." His words tailed off and he stood up to look around the room. "Puppy..." he said. "Why is everyone asleep?"

Fangs was right! Aside from us and Derek, who was still singing on the stage, everyone else in the room had fallen fast asleep. The customers, the DJ, even the snakes in the harpy's hairdo were all snoring away happily.

After Derek finished his song and took a bow, the audience slowly began to wake up again. They stretched and yawned.

"What's going on?" I asked Derek as he rejoined us.

The troll shrugged. "This always happens when I sing," he said. "People fall asleep."

I felt a smile creep across my face. "You're a genius," I said, clapping Derek on the back. "In fact, I think you've just found a way to get us into GLOVE."

"You think I sound like a police car?" Derek asked.

"No," I replied. "I said that your singing works like a siren's."

"Eh?"

Fangs and I were sitting in Derek's bedroom, trying to explain the details of my plan to get us inside GLOVE. The room was rather oddly decorated. The walls were painted in various shades of grey and had dozens of small stones and pebbles glued to them. Larger rocks were scattered across the bright red carpet, and the ceiling light gave the room a soft, scarlet glow.

The troll had been far too excited by his karaoke exploits to discuss my plan the night before. He'd sung loudly all the way home, sending everyone we passed on the street into a deep, restful slumber. Only Fangs and I were unaffected, and that was because of our anti-hypnotic implants. They were a standard issue for all MPl spies to stop us from being susceptible to most magic charms and spells. Thankfully, Derek hadn't questioned why we'd stayed awake.

"A siren is a kind of mermaid," Fangs explained. "They're very pretty."

"And deadly," I added. "Their voices have the ability to control people – just like yours does."

"You mean they make people fall asleep, too?" Derek asked.

"No," I said, "they lure ships onto the rocks by singing to the sailors."

"That doesn't sound very nice," said Derek.

"It isn't," I said. "But they promised to stop doing it when the supernatural equality laws came into force – in the same way that vampires agreed not to drink blood from living humans any more."

Fangs shuddered. "That was never a good way to get the stuff. Too messy – and blood's much better if you let it sit for a few hours before serving."

Derek was confused. "So ... I have to sing like a mermaid, but I'm not allowed to drink human blood?"

"You might have to explain the plan again, Puppy," Fangs said.

"OK," I said. "Like sirens, you have the ability to affect other people with your singing voice.

In your case, you can send people to sleep."

Derek nodded. "I know that. But how will that help get us into GLOVE?"

I smiled. "Well, let's say you make security guards fall asleep. Then we can sneak past them and help ourselves to whatever we want. Money, jewels, top-secret documents..."

Derek's eyes widened. "And THAT will get us membership of GLOVE?"

"Exactly."

Derek was clearly thinking hard. Finally he said, "Don't move," and pulled open a huge wardrobe. He began to root around inside.

Fangs whispered in my ear. "Are you sure this is a good idea?"

"We won't know until we try it, boss."

"But we're putting our trust in a troll who decorates his room to look like the inside of a volcano."

Before I could reply, Derek reappeared from

inside the wardrobe with a triumphant *"Voilà!"* He was wearing a black mask over his eyes and a tight yellow T-shirt with "DD" printed on the front of it. "I've been waiting for just the right moment to unveil my outfit. Now I *really* look like a super-villain. No one will forget the name Derek Dopper."

"Could this get any more embarrassing?" Fangs groaned.

"I've got T-shirts and masks for both of you, as well." Derek beamed.

"Yes, boss," I said. "Apparently, it can."

* * *

Derek had decided that he couldn't start his new career as a super-villain on an empty stomach. And so we went downstairs in our new T-shirts and masks. "I'll sit at the head of the table," said Derek. "You two should sit on either side of me in case anyone tries a sneak attack."

Fangs and I shared a glance. "A sneak attack?" he said.

Derek nodded. "Now I'm a major super-villain, there will be people wanting to topple me from my lofty perch and take over my organization. You two have to put yourselves in harm's way and block any attack aimed at me."

The door to the kitchen swung open and Derek's mum appeared, carrying a pan full of sausages. Well, I say pan *full* – there were three sausages. Three very small, lonely looking sausages.

"Look out," said Fangs in a mocking tone.

"Assault with a deadly sausage at three o'clock."

Doris carefully placed one sausage on each of our plates.

"Would it be possible to get an egg with that?" asked Fangs. "And some toast, if you don't mind."

Doris glared at him. "I haven't got time to waste making fancy breakfasts for the likes of you," she snapped. "Especially not dressed like that! I've got a bed and breakfast to run."

"Derek..." I said as Fangs pushed his sausage around his plate with a fork. "Have you ever sung to your mum?"

Derek blushed beneath his mask. "No, of course not."

"Well, why don't you try it now?"

It took a few moments for my idea to sink in, but eventually Derek smiled and began to sing *Zombie Feasting Time* in a soft, melodic voice.

"When I invite you round to dinner,
I just know that you'll get thinner,
You're losing precious pounds each
passing course..."

The effect was instant. Doris sank to the floor, sound asleep!

Derek placed a cushion under her head and smiled down at her as she

snored softly. "Sleeping beauty," he sighed.

Fangs pulled a face. "Well, *sleeping*, anyway... Now what say we upgrade this breakfast?"

Twenty minutes later, the three of us were tucking into a breakfast fit for a king: bacon, eggs, sausages, black pudding, tomatoes, mushrooms and more, all accompanied by a huge pot of tea. Doris was still sleeping happily on the carpet next to the sideboard, thanks to Derek keeping up the verses of his song in between mouthfuls of bacon and egg.

"Well," said Derek through a jawful of fried bread. "Now what?"

"Now we do something that will attract the attention of GLOVE," I said.

"But we can't just go out singing on the street and taking people's wallets once they're asleep," said Fangs. "That would be like busking for pennies. We need to go for something big."

I grinned. "I think I've got an idea..."

Thursday 0937 hours: **National Bank, Blackpool, UK**

We stepped out of the bright morning sun and into the cool, air-conditioned building of one of the town's busiest banks. Derek took one look at the queue of customers and the cashiers serving them, and froze.

"What's the matter?" I asked.

"There are so many people here," said Derek, clearly nervous. "What if they recognize us?"

Fangs tugged at the mask Derek had given him. "With these great disguises? No chance."

"But what if we get caught?"

"Doing what?" I asked. "All you're going to do is sing the customers and staff a little song. Fangs and I will do the rest. We are your henchmen, after all."

"You can't back out now," said Fangs. "You want your mum to be proud of you for making something of yourself, don't you?"

Derek nodded. He took a deep breath, and began to sing...

"I'll bite your spleen and sup your bile,
Chew your kidneys for a while,
Still got your appendix?
Baby, pass the sauce..."

One by one, the customers began to wobble, then their eyes fluttered closed and they sank to the floor, sound asleep. It took a few seconds longer for Derek's hypnotic voice to reach the cashiers on the other side of their glass screens but before long, they too were happily dozing on their desks.

I gestured for Derek to continue singing. We didn't want people waking up in the middle of our robbery. I pulled the Smartphone Cube had given me from my pocket and launched an app that would give me the electronic combinations for the locked doors that separated the cashiers from the rest of the bank.

Once they were open, we left Derek singing while Fangs pulled a black plastic bag out of his pocket and began to scoop handfuls of money from the cashier's drawers into it. I turned my attention to the bank's safe. After pressing one of my werewolf ears against the door, I turned the lock until I heard the clicks and whirrs which meant the steel rods inside were drawing back, one at a time.

If we weren't so thoroughly on the side of good, Fangs and I might have made a successful pair of bank robbers!

There was a final *SLAM!* as the safe door unlocked. I swung it open to reveal stacks

and stacks of money inside. There had to be over a million pounds here. This was sure to get us noticed by–

A leather glove clamped down over my mouth and the world turned black.

I woke to the rancid taste of chloroform in my mouth. I'd been knocked out!

I tried to sit up, only to discover that my arms and legs wouldn't move. I twisted my head to the side and found that I was flat on my back and strapped to a table. Fangs was similarly fixed to a table beside me – but he wasn't awake yet. I began to study my surroundings in an effort to work out where we were.

We were in a large, square room with

a circular window in the centre of each wall. The glass was cloudy, so I couldn't see out to get my bearings, but my sensitive werewolf ears were able to pick up the sound of heavy traffic. It was likely we were in a major town or city.

The ceiling rose high above us, and there was something circular up there. Not a window but some sort of opening. Chains snaked away from it to end at huge cogs and wheels that clicked and turned at a slow but regular pace.

CLUNK!

Could we be inside the belly of some incredible machine?

"No... I don't wanna wear the ballet shoes, Mum... The other vampires laugh at me..."

Fangs was starting to come round.

His head lolled from side to side and he was muttering to himself. "Hey ... that's *my* tutu! Get your own."

"Fangs," I hissed. "FANGS!"

"Wha– Wassa?" My boss's eyes flickered open and he turned towards me, struggling to focus. "Puppy?"

"It's me, boss," I said. "How are you feeling?"

Fangs groaned. "Like someone's been dancing inside my head."

"You mean like *ballet* dancing?"

"What?"

"Never mind."

Fangs tried to move and failed. Then he blinked hard and looked around the room. "Where did the bank go?"

"We were drugged," I said. "Chloroform."

"That explains why my mouth tastes like a pair of zombie's underpants," Fangs moaned. "Where are we now?"

"I could tell you exactly where you are," cried a tiny, high-pitched voice. "If I wanted to!"

"Shh," said Fangs. "Did you hear that? A kind

of squeaking noise? I think there may be a mouse in here."

"No, it's not a mouse," the voice said.

"There it is again! And it sounded like it was trying to talk that time."

There was a *click!*, and both our tables began to tilt, dropping us, feet first, until we were at a 45-degree angle. We were facing a large throne, silhouetted against one of the round windows.

CLUNK!

The machinery above us turned again.

"I must thank you for all your hard work," said the throne. No – there was something, or someone, sitting on it, although I couldn't see against the window's glare.

"Puppy," hissed Fangs. "I think I'm still suffering from the effects of the chloroform. The mouse just thanked us."

"I am NOT a mouse!"

A row of spotlights above the throne burst into life. For the first time, we could see who was talking. It was a leprechaun dressed in a green suit and hat. Shaggy red hair spilled out from under the hat's brim. It matched the beard that jutted from the creature's pointed chin.

I'd met several leprechauns during my time as a supernatural spy, but never one so tiny. He was standing on the seat of his luxurious chair, but didn't even reach over its arms.

"The name's Enigma," said my boss. "Fangs Enigma. Who are you?"

"I am the head of GLOVE," squeaked the leprechaun. "You may call me Mr Big."

Fangs erupted into laughter. "Mr Big? Hahahaha! I've picked things out of my nose that were bigger than you."

With a tiny howl of rage, Mr Big leapt down from his throne and ran towards us. It took a little while for him to reach us but when he did, he used the leather straps to help him climb onto Fangs's table. Then he strode confidently across Fangs's body to his chest and glared down at him.

"I would not advise such insolence in your position," the leprechaun said. "I am more dangerous than you think."

"I'll bet you are," said Fangs. "It would be quite easy to get something your size lodged in your throat and choke."

Mr Big screamed and slapped Fangs across the cheek with his miniature hand. It didn't leave a mark. "Perhaps you will be more impressed when you learn my real name," he growled. "I am Toby Shore."

I gasped. "The Dublin Dodger! You're the most wanted fugitive in Ireland – the only villain who can pick pockets from the *inside*." No wonder I hadn't recognized the villain when he first appeared. Toby Shore had never been captured in a photograph before. He was just too small.

"The very same," said Toby, taking a bow. "Although I have now moved my operations to a new location."

"Where are we?" demanded Fangs.

"You'll never guess."

CLUNK!

BONG!

It was the loudest noise I had ever heard in my life!

BONG!

Pain shot through my ears and stabbed daggers into my brain.

BONG!

I ground my teeth together to try to stop them from rattling.

BONG!

The noise was coming from that grey circle hanging from the ceiling. My eyes were watering so much that I found it difficult to focus on the shape... And then I knew where we were.

"We're inside the Elizabeth Tower," I cried. "The tower that houses Big Ben! That's the bell up there."

"But that means we're back in London," exclaimed Fangs. "Right across the river from MPI."

"Oh, all right. You can guess where we are," yelled Toby. "You still can't do anything to me."

"I can do anything I want," growled Fangs. "We're disavowed, which means we don't have to abide by the rules of MPI. When I get out of here—"

"Oh, please," the leprechaun said. "You haven't really been disavowed. It's all a pathetic trick to convince Derek Dopper to work with you."

"How could you know that?" I asked.

The leprechaun laughed. "I've been following you ever since I left the fake bomb under the

Speaker's chair in the Houses of Parliament."

"And you're small enough to get inside the mayor's house and Buckingham Palace. You could then open a door or window for one of your goons to leave a glove behind," I said.

"Don't forget MPl HQ." Toby smiled. "In fact, I was still inside Phlem's desk drawer when he showed you his glove."

"So there isn't a spy at MPl," I cried. "It was all you."

"OK," said Fangs. "We get it. You're tiny, and you know our cover story. That doesn't mean you can do anything about it."

"I don't need to do anything," said Toby. "It's happening already. As we speak, my fellow GLOVE members are gathering in the rose garden behind Ten Downing Street. It's going to be quite a concert."

"Concert?" I asked. "What concert?"

"We were planning to rob a few banks together but, thanks to you, GLOVE can now do so much more! Your friend Derek is going to visit Number Ten to sing the prime minister and all his staff to sleep," the leprechaun explained. "Then we can help ourselves to anything we want belonging to his government. Money, armies, and state secrets! Anything."

"You must be out of your tiny mind," Fangs said.

Toby's cheeks flushed as red as his beard. "SILENCE!" He ran back down Fangs's body and leapt off the table. After a moment, I could hear the sound of something heavy scraping over the stone ground behind us. I strained my neck and was surprised to see the leprechaun dragging a pot of gold across the room.

"By this time tomorrow, we shall have everything we desire – and you two gave us the means to do it."

"But why?" I asked. "You don't need the money, not with a stash of gold like that."

Toby emerged from beneath Fangs's table and smiled. "Oh, that's not spending gold," he said. "That's magic gold! Watch..." He clicked his fingers and a rainbow of light poured in through the clock face opposite us and arched towards the pot.

But this was no ordinary rainbow.

It began to burn into the end of the table between my boss's legs, and to slowly creep up towards his body.

"I'm afraid I have to *split* now," said Toby. "But then you'll be doing much the same in a few minutes' time, Agent Enigma."

The rainbow had burned up the table to knee level now. Multi-coloured sparks began to rain down over Fangs's body.

"You're insane!" Fangs shrieked.

"Goodbye, Fangs Enigma."

Then, with the tiniest of evil laughs, the leprechaun was gone.

Thursday 1611 hours: **GLOVE HQ, Big Ben, London, UK**

"This is bad!" cried Fangs as the rainbow cut higher and higher into the table beneath him. "I'm going to end up *half* the vampire I used to be."

I stretched my neck out as far as I could and blew on the coloured flames, but it had no effect. "There's nothing I can do, boss," I said. "The end of the rainbow is forcing its way to the pot of gold."

"Which is where?"

I glanced beneath Fangs's table. "Right below your head." I pulled and pulled against the straps holding my wrists down, trying to break free – even if I couldn't save Fangs, I wanted to hold his hand, at least. But it was no good. I was bound too tightly. "Thanks for everything, boss," I said, forcing myself to smile. "It's been brilliant."

"Better than that, Puppy." Fangs winked at me. "It's been *fang*-tastic."

Then the door burst open and we turned our heads to see ... Phlem's secretary, Miss Bile!

"What are you doing here?" Fangs cried.

"SHAVING YOU!" screeched the banshee.

"I'm not sure this is the best time for a shave, actually," Fangs said.

"She means she's here to *save* us," I said. "Quick, Miss Bile, slide the pot of gold out from beneath Fangs."

The banshee moved faster than I imagined anyone her age could. She sprinted across the room and dived beneath Fangs's table. I heard the pot slide across the floor and the rainbow changed direction. And not a moment too soon – Fangs's trousers had begun to sizzle!

"Colour me impressed," sighed Fangs, slumping back against the table.

While my boss caught his breath, Miss Bile fished a pair of nail scissors from her handbag and began to cut through the leather straps binding my wrists and ankles.

"How did you know we were here?" I asked.

The crone blushed. "I SHNUCK A TRACKING DEVISHE IN FANGSH'S CLOAK WHEN I HEARD PHLEM WAS SHACKING YOU. I COULDN'T LET MY SHWEETHEART JUSHT WALK OUT OF MY LIFE."

Finally, my wrists were free and I sat up to help Miss Bile unstrap my feet.

"Look out! Behind you!" cried Fangs.

An imp, dressed all in black, was running across the room towards us. It must have been one of Mr Big's goons. I was still fastened to the table by one of my ankles, so I couldn't move. Miss Bile swung out with her handbag, hitting the henchman square in the face and knocking him out cold with a *CLANG!*

"What have you got in there?" I asked.

Miss Bile shrugged and pulled out a large stapler. "I KEEP OFFICE SHTATIONERY WITH ME AT ALL TIMESH IN CASHE I FIND SHOMETHING THAT NEEDSH FILING."

I could hear footsteps climbing the stairs outside the clock room – more henchmen! As soon as I was free of my bonds, I hurried to slam and lock the door while Miss Bile untied Fangs.

"Sounds like there are more of Shore's goons out there," I said. "And it's the only way down."

"One thing you should know about situations like this, Puppy, is that there's *always* another way down." Fangs grabbed one of the metal chains that hung from the ceiling.

I glanced from my boss to the clock face and back again. "You don't mean...?"

Fangs's eyes sparkled behind his sunglasses. "You betcha." He grinned as he threw identical lengths of chain to Miss Bile and me.

So as a horde of evil imps tried to break down the door, Fangs, Miss Bile and I wrapped the chains tightly around our waists. Then we ran at the glass clock face and jumped straight through it.

We slammed against the outside of the tower a few metres below the number six on the clock – just as the door gave way in the room above. We'd each have some bruises to show for our actions, but that was the least of our worries.

"Breezy up here, isn't it?" cried Fangs.

"Breezy" was a bit of an understatement. The wind blew hard against my fur, and I was forced to plunge my claws into the brick to ensure I stayed in one place. I glanced over my shoulder, and found that I could see across Parliament Square and along Whitehall to Downing Street itself. Toby Shore could already be there, convincing

Derek to put everyone in the government to sleep.

A dozen or more tiny faces appeared through the broken glass above us. We had to go now.

"Ready?" I yelled against the gale.

"Ready as I'll ever be," Fangs called back.

"THISH ISH FANTASHTIC!" bellowed Miss Bile excitedly.

Then we released our grips on the chains.

We fell, spinning over and over like yo-yos as the chains unwound. The ground – what I could see of it as I tumbled – came rushing up to meet us. We plummeted faster and faster, spun quicker and quicker, screamed louder and louder, and then we ran out of chain.

We fell the final ten metres and bounced on the awning of the House of Commons coffee bar. The material ripped gradually, slowing our descent enough to allow us to survive the drop. We landed on the tables and chairs below, spraying members of parliament and their aides with coffee and cakes.

"It's raining spies today," said Fangs to one alarmed MP. "Just pop your suit in at the dry cleaners and claim it on expenses later."

Then we were off, leaping over the security gate and racing down Whitehall towards Downing Street. We dodged between tourists until we arrived at the metal gates that protected the most important road in Britain. The police officer on duty was slumped against the steel bars, out cold – and the gates were open!

"They're already here," I cried.

We jumped over the sleeping policeman and ran along Downing Street. The door to Number 10 was open as well. We dashed through the house to the gardens at the back of the building, where we skidded to a halt and ducked down behind the bushes to avoid being seen.

Derek was there, along with Mr Big and the other four villains signed up to GLOVE: General Rot, Carlos Trumpet, Arnold Goose and Betty Flame. These were the biggest names in super-villainy – and they *all* had a pack of rugged henchmen or -women with them. There must have been over 100 people crowded on the lawn, and they were each wearing a single black glove.

Derek was at the centre of the group, gazing up at the first-floor windows of 10 Downing Street, where Prime Minister Sir Hugh Jands was standing at the window. He was singing to the head of the British government!

"Chewin' on you, you're tastin' good,
Gnawing your bones and drinkin' your blood,
Baby, you're a zombie meal for one..."

Sir Hugh Jands wobbled, then his eyes closed and he fell backwards, sound asleep.

"That's everyone inside the building asleep," said Toby Shore, rubbing his tiny hands together with glee. "Now then, who wants what?"

"I'll have an aircraft carrier," cried General Rot.

"I've always fancied being the king of somewhere," announced Arnold Goose. "The Isle of Wight, maybe?"

"They must all be wearing earplugs," I hissed. "Otherwise, they'd be snoring by now, as well."

"WHAT'SH THE PLAN?" asked Miss Bile. The secretary was still awake, so I presumed she had anti-hypnotic implants just like us.

Fangs took a deep breath. "Well," he said. "There are over a hundred bad guys. Many of them are henchmen, highly trained in martial arts ... and we've got a werewolf, a banshee and a vampire with a pair of singed trousers."

"Could be a tough one, boss," I agreed.

"Not at all," said Fangs. "Because we've got the element of surprise."

Miss Bile looked puzzled. "WE DO?"

Fangs nodded. "They'll all be *surprised* that we attacked them when the odds are so badly stacked against us. Ready? Charge!"

Fangs pulled us through the hedge – and then tripped over his own feet. We all landed *SPLAT!*

"Stop what you are doing," Fangs shouted, picking himself up. "You are all under arrest."

Everyone laughed.

"I'm not joking," Fangs warned.

Toby Shore looked us up and down, which from his perspective, was mainly up. "The sad part is, I know you're not joking. You really think you can stop us." He looked from super-villain to super-villain. "Who wants to capture the infamous Fangs Enigma and his pesky sidekick?"

Four black-gloved hands shot up into the air. Toby made a big show of deciding which bad guy to choose. "Carlos," he said finally to a skeleton dressed all in white. "What would you do with a couple of MPI secret agents?"

"It's-a simples." Carlos Trumpet beamed. "I will-a grind them up to use as-a pig food on my farm back home."

"Then they're all yours," said Toby.

Carlos nodded to his batch of goons, who were also dressed in white. The henchmen grabbed Fangs, Miss Bile and me easily, before dragging us towards the exit at the far end of the garden. Beyond the gate, I could just make out the shape of a large white van. I had to do something – and quickly.

"Derek," I shouted. "These people are just using you."

"No, they're not," he sang back. *"They're letting me join GLOVE. They're giving me everything I have ever wanted."*

I shook my head. "No," I said. "It's the other way round. I don't think you really want to be a super-villain. I just think you want your mum to be proud of you."

Derek's bottom lip quivered. *"I like calling bingo,"* he sang. *"But she said it wasn't a real career."*

"Of course it's not a real career," interrupted Toby Shore. "Reading numbers off a bag of coloured balls? Stay with us, Derek! Sing for us, and you can have any job you want. Maybe we'll let you be prime minister! The current one appears to have fallen asleep on the job."

Derek smiled. "Prime minister...?"

"Imagine how proud your mum will be then." Toby grinned.

"Don't listen to him, Derek," warned Fangs.

"Enough!" roared Toby. "Carlos, keep your prisoners under control. I don't want to hear another word out of them. Now, where were we? Who hasn't got anything yet?"

"Me," said Betty Flame, much to the excitement of her gang, a group of vicious-looking mummies. "I'd like the medical histories of the royal family. I want to blackmail them into handing me the keys to Buckingham Palace."

"I don't think that will be happening today," glugged a voice. I looked up to see a slimy green figure push its way out of the bushes and into the garden.

"Phlem!" I cried. And he wasn't alone! With him were Cube, Doctor Olga Nowkoff, MPl's chief surgeon, and Special Agents Osiris Tut, Winnie Bag and Wade Soul. Jeff the security ogre was there too, along with various technicians, lab assistants and computer operators.

The whole of MPl had come to help us!

"How did you find us?" asked Fangs.

Phlem arched a green eyebrow. "A broken clock face, three figures jumping out of Big Ben and a trashed coffee shop? It couldn't be anyone else, Agent Enigma." He turned to glower down at Toby Shore. "Now, I believe Fangs told you that you were all under arrest..."

"Never!" barked the leprechaun. "Attack!"

Every bad guy and MPl employee sprang forward at once.

It was an incredible battle – one that would go down in MPl history.

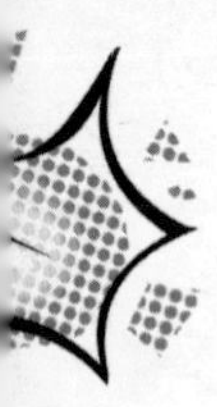

Doctor Nowkoff hurled syringes like darts at Betty Flame's gang of mummies, who fell to the ground, unconscious. "The strongest sleeping potion I've ever concocted." Doctor Nowkoff winked at me as she spun to stab yet another girly goon and knock her out.

Cube, meanwhile, was firing pink goo from a fountain pen. The gunk solidified over Arnold Goose's assistants, slowing their movements until they dried to look like sugar-coated statues.

The lab technicians were throwing lassos made from computer power cables. They had captured General Rot and his men. One of the techies I knew only by the codename XD ducked beneath the mêlée to help me to my feet.

"Are you OK, miss?" he asked as he pulled me to one side. Another of Doctor Nowkoff's syringes whizzed past us.

"I'm fine, thanks," I said. Then I noticed that Toby Shore was climbing the rose trellis on the back wall of 10 Downing Street. There was no way I was going to let him escape. I tried to fight my way through the crowd, but my path was blocked by Jeff the security guard. He was knocking two of the bad guys' heads together, adding to the growing pile of unconscious bodies in the middle of the lawn.

I looked round for my boss, but couldn't make him out in the mêlée. But then I heard the overpowering screech of Miss Bile: "FANGSH! BEHIND YOU!"

I turned to see Fangs spin round. Three of Carlos Trumpet's goons were racing towards him. He swung out a fist, as did Miss Bile and Phlem. All three villains hit the ground at the same time.

I looked up. Toby Shore was just below the roof of Number 10. I raced across the lawn towards Miss Bile, my feet slipping on the muddy grass. As I skidded past the secretary, I plunged my paw into her handbag and pulled out the large office stapler.

"Fangs," I cried. "Time for me to go *up* in the world."

With a grin, both my boss and Agent Osiris Tut grabbed my legs and threw me as hard as they could into the air.

I reached the escaping leprechaun just as he was about to climb over the gutter. Clinging to the gutter for support, I slammed the stapler into the material of his suit four times.

KATHUNK! KATHUNK! KATHUNK! KATHUNK!

I fell back down towards the ground, where Fangs caught me in his arms. We both looked up to see Toby Shore stapled hard and fast to the wooden trellis. The miniature mob boss was screaming with rage, but he wasn't going anywhere!

"Are you going to arrest him, boss?" I asked.

Fangs pulled off his yellow T-shirt and winked at me from behind his sunglasses. "There's no rush, Puppy." He grinned. "Toby Shore will remain *stationery* for the time being."

CASE CLOSED

SIGNED: Agent Puppy Brown

Thursday 2157 hours: **South Bank, London, UK**

"Fifty-two... Seventeen... Thirty-six...

And a portion of fried rice as well, please." Special Agent Fangs Enigma handed the Chinese takeaway menu back to the woman behind the counter and joined his sidekick and best friend, Puppy Brown, on the bench in the waiting area.

"I'm looking forward to this," he said. "Haven't eaten since breakfast in Blackpool this morning. I'm famished."

"Well," said Puppy. "I might just have a little something to keep you going until the food is ready." She reached into her pocket and pulled out a red-and-white striped candy stick wrapped in clear plastic.

"A stick of Blackpool rock!" cried Fangs. "And look – it says 'MP1'." He began to suck away happily on the treat.

Puppy grinned. "I had Cube knock one up in the lab while you were locking Toby Shore and his fellow GLOVE members in the cells," she said.

Fangs pulled the rock from his mouth. "Cube made this? It's not another one of his gadgets, is it? It's not going to expand in my stomach and turn me into the fattest vampire alive, or something mad like that?"

Puppy laughed. "No, it's just a plain stick of rock, although it is bad for your fangs."

"You sound like my mum." Fangs grinned. "Even worse, you sound like Derek's mum."

"I wonder how he's getting on," Puppy mused.

"Let's go and find out, shall we?" said Fangs. He collected their bag of takeaway meals from the counter and the secret agents stepped out into the cool night air.

Just then, Big Ben began to chime. *BONG!* The pair glanced over to where workers had begun to replace the broken clock face.

After crossing the street, Puppy located a hidden sensor in the back wall of the building opposite the Chinese restaurant and pressed her fur-covered palm against it. This was another of the secret entrances to MP1 Headquarters. Blue lights whooshed across the metal, and then a computerized voice sounded:

"Access granted. Welcome back, Agent Brown."

A door slid open just long enough for Fangs and Puppy to slip inside unnoticed – where they found themselves face to face with a large troll in an MP1 security uniform.

"You'll have to put that bag through the scanner, sir," said Derek Dopper. "And did you remember to get my prawn crackers?"

"Got them," said Fangs, sitting the food on

the conveyor belt. "But you can't eat while you're on duty."

Puppy grinned.

After a personal call from Sir Hugh Jands, Phlem had agreed to offer Derek a full pardon for his attempt at villainy in return for coming to work at MP1, and allowing the organization to use his special singing voice on missions from time to time. The PM thought the troll's voice could be used to knock out enemy agents without any nasty after-effects. Derek had excitedly agreed.

Of course, it was a *small* possibility that the PM's call might have been made by a certain Agent Fangs Enigma, using Cube's voice scrambler to disguise himself as Sir Hugh, but Phlem wasn't to know that...

Jeff the security ogre stepped out of his office. "All right then, Derek," he said. "You can take your break now."

"Great!" Derek grinned, slipping off his peaked cap. "A new job AND a break to eat my dinner!

This is the best day ever."

"How's the MP1 flat?" asked Puppy as she collected the bag of food from the scanner.

"It's brilliant," enthused Derek. "My mum's there now, cleaning it for me. She says she might even stay with me in London for a while until I'm settled in."

The trio reached Phlem's office where Phlem, Cube and Miss Bile were waiting for them.

"FANGSH," screeched Miss Bile, her voice quivering. "IT'SH YOU!"

"It is indeed, Miss Bile," soothed the world's greatest vampire spy. "I wonder – could you get me a drink? Milk, with just a drop of human blood."

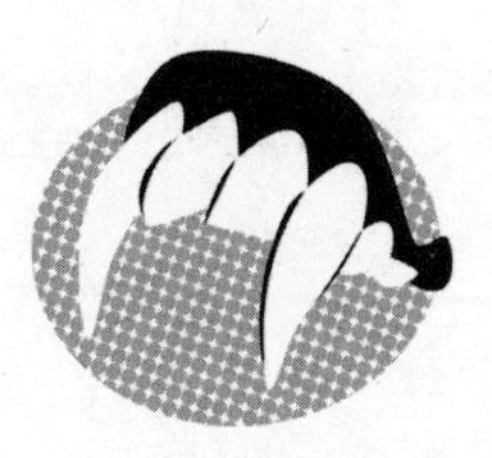

ABOUT THE AUTHOR

TOMMY DONBAVAND was born and brought up in Liverpool and has worked at numerous careers that have included clown, actor, theatre producer, children's entertainer, drama teacher, storyteller and writer. He is the author of the popular thirteen-book series Scream Street. His other books include *Zombie!*; *Wolf*; *Uniform*; and Doctor Who: *Shroud of Sorrow*. His non-fiction books for children and their parents, *Boredom Busters* and *Quick Fixes for Bored Kids*, have helped him to become a regular guest on radio stations around the UK and he also writes for a number of magazines, including *Creative Steps* and Scholastic's *Junior Education*.

Tommy lives in Lancashire with his family. He is a huge fan of all things Doctor Who, plays blues harmonica and makes a mean balloon poodle. He sees sleep as a waste of good writing time.

You can find out more about Tommy and his books at his website: www.tommydonbavand.com

Visit the Fangs website at: www.fangsvampirespy.co.uk

TEST YOUR SECRET-AGENT

Spot the Difference (There are eight to spot.)

SKILLS WITH THESE PUZZLES!

Derek Dopper Facts

How well do you know this wannabe villain?
Answer these questions and find out!

1) Where does Derek live?

2) What song does Derek sing at Bassey's Karaoke Bar?

3) What is Derek's dream home?

Answers

Derek Dopper Facts

Blackpool; *Zombie Feasting Time*; a hollowed-out volcano.

UNLOCK SECRET MISSION FILES!

Want to gain access to highly classified MPl files?

Complete the crossword below, and then enter

the password (the letters in the grey boxes) at

WWW.FANGSVAMPIRESPY.CO.UK/MISSION6

Across

2. What creature is Mr Big? (10)
4. What is Phlem's secretary called? (4, 4)
6. What does Derek use to tie up Fangs and Puppy? (10)
8. What is Mr Big's real name? (4, 5)
10. Where are GLOVE's Headquarters? (3, 3)
12. What "explodes" from the bomb? (5)

Down

1. Who is the skeleton super-villain in GLOVE? (6, 7)
3. Complete the name of Mrs Dopper's B&B. _ _ _ _ _ _ _ _ _ Dreams (9)
5. What colour is Derek's super-villain T-shirt? (6)
7. What game do Puppy and Fangs play at Bingo Bongo? (5)
9. What is the name of MPl's security ogre? (4)